Rock Climbing

A Level Two Reader

By Cynthia Klingel and Robert B. Noyed

The Child's World®

Rock climbing is an exciting sport. It may look scary, but it is fun.

You need the right gear to be safe. A helmet protects your head.

You wear a harness on your waist. The harness is snug around your legs and waist.

A long rope is tied to the harness. The rope keeps you from falling.

9

10

You look at the rock-climbing wall before starting. Now it is time to climb.

The wall has places to put your hands and feet. There is not always a good spot.

13

14

Climbing can be harder than it looks. You have to think about where to put your hands and feet.

Your foot might slip off the wall. That's why you have a rope!

18

You reach the top of the wall. Now you need to get down. You are lowered by the rope.

You make it to the bottom of the wall. You are ready to climb again!

20

Index

To Find Out More

Books

Hyden, Tom. *Rock Climbing Is for Me*. Minneapolis: Lerner Publications Co., 1984.

Radlauer, Ed. *Some Basics about Rock Climbing*. Chicago: Children's Press, 1981.

Smith, Ian. *Rock Climbing*. New York: Barron's Educational Series, 1999.

Web Sites

Friends of Pinnacles
http://www.pinnacles.org
An organization dedicated to working with the National Park Service to preserve rock climbing and the environment at Pinnacles National Monument.

Note to Parents and Educators

Welcome to The Wonders of Reading™! These books provide text at three different levels for beginning readers to practice and strengthen their reading skills. Additionally, the use of nonfiction text provides readers the valuable opportunity to *read to learn*, not just to learn to read.

These leveled readers allow children to choose books at their level of reading confidence and performance. Level One books offer beginning readers simple language, word choice, and sentence structure as well as a word list. Level Two books feature slightly more difficult vocabulary, longer sentences, and longer total text. In the back of each Level Two book are an index and a list of books and Web sites for finding out more information. Level Three books continue to extend word choice and length of text. In the back of each Level Three book are a glossary, an index, and a list of books and Web sites for further research.

State and national standards in reading and language arts emphasize using nonfiction at all levels of reading development. The Wonders of Reading™ fill the historical void in nonfiction material for the primary grade readers with the additional benefit of a leveled text.

About the Authors

Cindy Klingel has worked as a high school English teacher and an elementary teacher. She is currently the curriculum director for a Minnesota school district. Writing children's books is another way for her to continue her passion for sharing the written word with children. Cindy Klingel is a frequent visitor to the children's section of bookstores and enjoys spending time with her many friends, family, and two daughters.

Bob Noyed started his career as a newspaper reporter. Since then, he has worked in communications and public relations for more than fourteen years for a Minnesota school district. He enjoys writing books for children and finds that it brings a different feeling of challenge and accomplishment from other writing projects. He is an avid reader who also enjoys music, theater, traveling, and spending time with his wife, son, and daughter.

Readers should remember…
All sports carry a certain amount of risk. To reduce your risk while rock climbing, climb at your own experience level, wear all safety equipment, and use care and common sense. The publisher and author will take no responsibility or liability for injuries resulting from rock climbing.

Published by The Child's World®, Inc.
PO Box 326
Chanhassen, MN 55317-0326
800-599-READ
www.childsworld.com

With special thanks to the Daulton family, David Hudson, and Hidden Peak at the Lakeshore Academy of Chicago for providing the modeling and location for this book.

Photo Credits
All photos © Flanagan Publishing Services/Romie Flanagan

Project Coordination: Editorial Directions, Inc.
Photo Research: Alice K. Flanagan

Library of Congress Cataloging-in-Publication Data
Klingel, Cynthia Fitterer.
Rock climbing / by Cynthia Klingel and Robert B. Noyed.
p. cm. — (Wonder books)
"A level two reader" —Cover.
Summary: Briefly describes rock climbing, how it's done, the equipment used, and how to stay safe.
Includes bibliographical references (p.) and index.
ISBN 1-56766-817-8 (lib. bdg. : alk. paper)
1. Rock climbing—Juvenile literature.   [1. Rock climbing.]
I. Noyed, Robert B.   II. Title.   III. Wonder books (Chanhassen, Minn.)

GV200.2 .K45   2000
796.52'23—dc21   99-057724